Dot to Dot...

Words by Malcolm Cossons
and Pictures by Neil Stevens

First published in 2013 in hardcover in the United States of America by
Thames & Hudson Inc., 500 Fifth Avenue, New York, New York 10110

thamesandhudsonusa.com

Library of Congress Catalog Card Number 2012951717

ISBN 978-0-500-65015-8

Printed and bound in China by Everbest Printing Co. Ltd

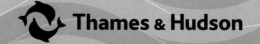
Thames & Hudson

This is **Dot**.

She's not the only **Dot**.

Dot's grandma is also called **Dot**.

And the special thing is, they share the same birthday!

More than anything in the world, **Dot** wanted
to spend her birthday with **Grandma Dot**.
But **Dot** lives in **London** . . .

. . . and **Grandma Dot** lives in **New York**,
far away across the ocean.

Dot had an idea. She would make a fabulous card to send to **Grandma Dot** . . .

But she was so busy cutting, sticking and painting that she missed the post.

Now her card would never get there in time for **Grandma Dot's** birthday!

Dot decided to take the card to **New York** herself.

She gathered everything that could fly,

but even with springs on her feet,

she couldn't bounce across the ocean.

So **Dot** decided to ask some animals to carry her card to **New York**.

She asked a blackbird,

she asked some bees,

she even asked a snail,
but it was too far for
them to cross the ocean.

Next, **Dot** tried to dig a tunnel **under** the ocean.
But by teatime, she hadn't even left her garden.

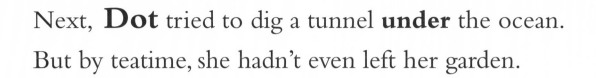

Their birthday was the very next day, and **Dot** didn't know how she would get her card to **Grandma Dot** in time!

Early the next morning, a commotion woke **Dot** up.

A big, red London bus pulled up outside her front door!

Out spilled
Dot's family
from across
the world,
but best of all . . .

...Grandma Dot!

Happy birthday, **Dot!**

. . . Do!

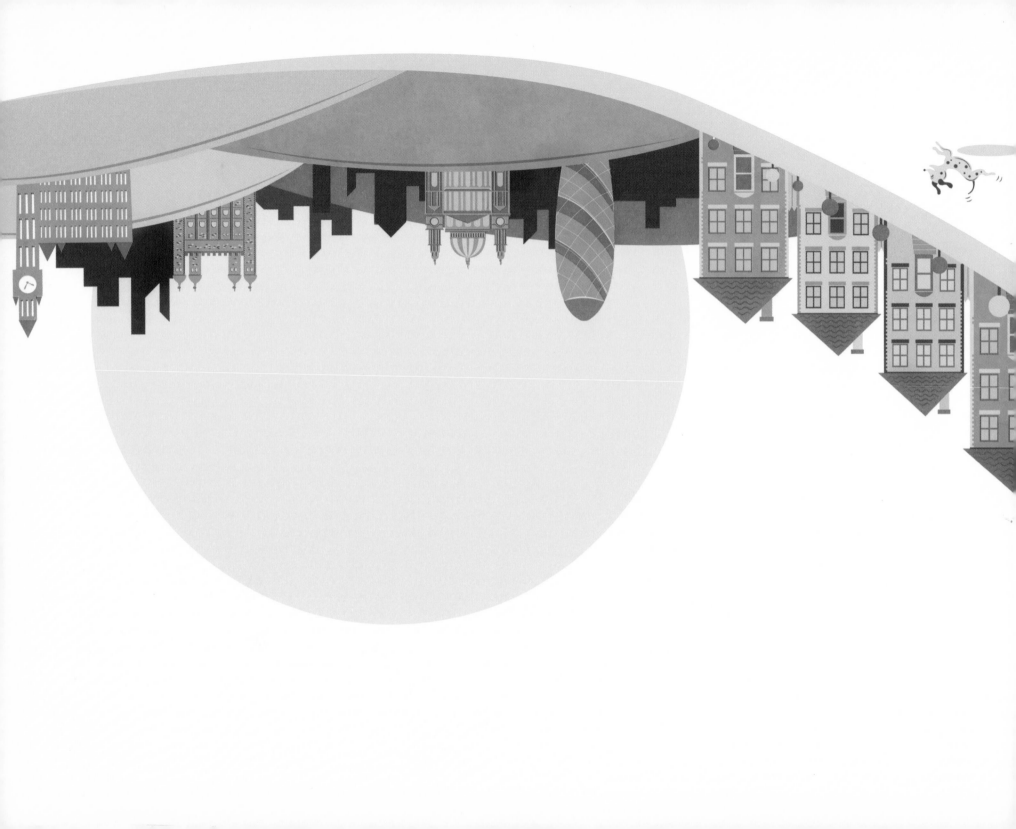

. . . **London**—just in time for **Dot's** birthday!
With all their luggage, packages and presents,
Grandma Dot and her family filled a whole
double-decker bus. They raced across town and all piled out.

A door opened and out came . . .

They got lost in the ancient ruins,

ate gelato, then rushed

to catch the plane to . . .

. . . **Rome** in **Italy**,
where they picked up two more of
Grandma Dot's grandsons.

. . . **Mumbai** in **India**, where they picked up two of **Grandma Dot's** grandsons.

They danced at the Bollywood film studios, went to the bazaar,
then dashed to catch a plane to . . .

They explored the Forbidden City,

went to the market, then

hurried to catch the plane to . . .

First, **Grandma Dot** flew to **Beijing** in **China**,
where three more of her granddaughters live.
She asked them to come to **London**, too.

. . . and **Dot** lives in **London**, far away across the ocean.

Grandma Dot decided to pay **Dot** a surprise visit. But there was only one plane ticket left—going the long way round to **London**! This gave **Grandma Dot** an idea . . .

More than anything in the world, **Grandma Dot** wanted to spend her birthday with **Dot**.
But **Grandma Dot** lives in **New York** . . .

This is **Grandma Dot**.

She's not the only **Dot**.

Dot's granddaughter is also called **Dot**.

And—would you believe it—they share exactly the same birthday!

Dot to Dot...

Words by Malcolm Cossons and pictures by Neil Stevens

Thames & Hudson